Pitch and Hasty Check It Out

A
Richard Jackson
Book

Pitch and Hasty Check It Out

by ERIC DELEON

ORCHARD BOOKS · New York & London
A division of Franklin Watts, Inc.

Orchard Books, 387 Park Avenue South
New York, New York 10016

Orchard Books Great Britain, 10 Golden Square
London W1R 3AF England

Orchard Books Australia, 14 Mars Road
Lane Cove, New South Wales 2066

Orchard Books Canada, 20 Torbay Road
Markham Ontario 23P 1G6

Orchard Books is a division of Franklin Watts, Inc.

Manufactured in the United States of America
Book design by Mina Greenstein
The text of this book is set in 12 pt. Caledonia
10 9 8 7 6 5 4 3 2 1

Library of Congress Cataloging-in-Publication Data
Deleon, Eric.
Pitch and Hasty check it out/ Eric Deleon.
"A Richard Jackson book."
Summary: Two boys investigating a mysterious voice coming from a pinball
machine become involved with a parrot-smuggling ring.
ISBN 0-531-05768-2.   ISBN 0-531-08368-3 (lib. bdg.)
[1. Smuggling—Fiction. 2. Mystery and detective stories.]
I. Title.   PZ7.D38317Pi 1988 [Fic]—dc19   88-1483   CIP AC

This book is dedicated to Holly,
with love

Pitch and Hasty
Check It Out

1.

PITCH LOCKED his bike in the stand and hesitated before going into the mall. He brushed the dirt from his pants and T-shirt, hair and back and bottom. His front tire had gotten hung up in the loose sand by Keerson's Realty and he had done a forward somersault over the bars that left his elbows skinned. He checked them to make sure they had stopped bleeding.

He was at the mall because his best friend Hasty had called him the night before to tell him about a new video game in the Video Arcade.

"It's called Total Devastator," Hasty had said. "I saw it on television. You battle for control of the whole galaxy and if you lose Earth becomes dust. Unless you put in another quarter. You've got to try it. I'll meet you there tomorrow morning."

"I don't know. . . ."

"Come on—you've got to hit one sooner or later."

That was the problem, Pitch thought, standing by the bike rack at the entry to the mall. Right there was the problem. He just wasn't good at video games. He'd tried all of them. Every time he got an extra quarter, or even when it wasn't extra, he seemed to be dropping it in a video game.

And he probably held the record for the shortest time played for a quarter. Just under five seconds. He had worked it out on a calculator and figured it was costing him a hundred and eighty dollars an hour to prove he was a ten-year-old klutz.

There was just something not connected between his brain and his hand when it came to video games. Part of it was that he thought things out too much. You couldn't take time to think with video games, and he always tried to think things out before doing them. He wasn't sure why he did it, because it seemed to get him into all sorts of trouble.

Take his nickname, for instance. It came from just thinking things out. He had heard when he was eight that there was something called terminal velocity; that nothing could fall faster than a hundred and twenty miles an hour or something. Pitch thought it meant that nothing could go faster than that, no matter what, unless it had a motor, like a jet.

Then he saw a baseball pitcher during a game on television and they said his pitches were close to a hundred miles an hour. So Pitch thought about it and decided to see if he could get a baseball to move over a hundred and twenty miles an hour.

He went to the playground at school where there was room, taped a long string to a baseball and started whirling it around, letting the string out a bit with each circle. When the string got out to twenty feet or so, the ball was really smoking. He was pretty sure it was over a hundred and twenty—everything was blurred as he went around and he felt like throwing up—when the string broke.

Even then it would have been all right except that luck stepped in, bad luck, and the whistling ball blew a clean, perfectly round hole in the windshield of Mr. Patterson the principal's car sitting in the school parking lot.

Two hundred and seventeen dollars and forty-seven cents worth of hole. Pitch's father had paid it and Pitch had worked it off—it seemed like for the rest of his life—doing chores around the house. When Hasty heard about it he had smiled and said, "Way to go, Pitch."

And so his nickname was born.

Because he thought things out. And now here he was again, on the edge of spending a hundred and eighty dollars an hour to prove he couldn't do video games. He was still hesitating, thinking he might slip away, when Hasty came out of the mall. He nailed Pitch right away.

"I knew you were here. Come on—you've got to try this game. I've only been here half an hour and I'm already up to the seventh level."

Pitch smiled. Of course he was up to the seventh level. He was probably born at the seventh level. Hasty always got so excited about things.

"Man, they come at you from all sides in devastator modules that can go in and out of hyperwarp and you have to rotate your firing capsule to meet them all and then there's this one that's invisible, see, or that you can't see, see, because it's invisible, see, and you have to defend against him while you're rotating your capsule taking on the other four. . . ."

And he took Pitch by the arm and dragged him into the mall still talking, and Pitch thought, well, it can't be that bad to at least give it a try.

Which was just about the biggest mistake of his life.

2.

"I KNEW I shouldn't have done it."

Pitch watched the screen flash the game over light. He didn't break his record. In his first run-through with the Total Devastator, Pitch lasted almost twenty-seven seconds before he got vaporized. But it wasn't a quarter, either, it was fifty cents, so he still zinged in at close to sixty dollars an hour.

"I'll be at the pinball machines."

He left Hasty working for level eight and went to the back of the video game area where old Petey kept the antique pinball machines. They were the ones with five balls, and he got more enjoyment out of them. Also more time.

He dropped a quarter in the Motocross Game pinball, fired a ball, and got busy with the flippers. More my speed, he thought. He kept the first ball in play for quite a while—almost a minute—and was just getting ready to shoot the second one when the voice stopped him.

"Something wrong. Something wrong."

Pitch held back on the plunger. He thought he knew the voice but didn't want to seem to be a snoop. It sounded like the voice of a young boy but it also sounded very worried and strange, kind of high pitched, and he couldn't figure out where it was coming from.

It seemed to be inside his head, or coming right out of the pinball machine, a kind of metallic voice. He waited for something else, but a half a minute went by and he heard no more. He looked around the pinball area to see if anybody else heard it, but there was nobody standing close to him. Pitch released another ball, caught it on a flipper, got a lucky bounce and hit the five-thousand-point hole.

That meant a free game. He actually got a free game. Wait until he told Hasty.

"Something wrong. Something wrong." The voice was a bit louder this time, and very tinny, and came right out of the middle of the motocross rider's face on the glass back of the pinball machine.

"I beg your pardon?"

Pitch felt only a little silly, talking to the back of a pinball machine, especially being so polite. He wondered if a pinball could be haunted. Maybe there was a ghost. The ghost of the pinball? Come on, he thought, get real.

"Did you say something to me?"

Again, there was no further talk, no sound except for the noise of the video game area to his rear. He stared at the middle of the motocross rider intently. Maybe there was a speaker in there, maybe this was some kind of joke. Once more he looked around the room, but nobody was looking at him or seemed to notice him. Hasty was still at the Total Devastator game, twisting and turning with his hand action on the joystick. Hmmm. He turned back to the pinball machine.

Maybe it was the ball that triggered the speaker or something. He put another ball up, released the plunger and fired it out. Then he looked up at the glass. Nothing. The ball bounced twice, then dropped like it had been shot down through the obstacles into the return hole. A wasted shot. And no voice.

When another minute passed and he still heard no voice, he pushed the button for his free game, jacked a ball up and fired it. It started to work down through the bumpers, and he half expected to hear the voice, waited for it, and missed the ball, which dropped through into the return.

He put yet another ball up. He would have to pay more attention. He released it, worked the flippers, tipped his hips, pushed on the machine and managed to keep the ball in play, working it back up through the bumpers, really getting into it, maybe going to get another free game. . . .

"Something wrong. Something wrong."

"Arrgh!" Pitch threw his hands up. "All right, all right. I've had enough. Whoever that is, stop it."

"What's happening?" Hasty walked up in back of him just as the ball dropped into the return. "Who are you yelling at?"

Pitch turned, saw Hasty and pointed at the back of the pinball machine.

"Him. I'm talking to him."

"Who?"

"Him. The man in the machine. Didn't you hear him?"

Hasty studied the glass back, then looked at Pitch. "Have you been holding your breath too long?"

"I tell you I heard a voice. I really did."

"What did it say?"

Pitch thought a moment. "I think it was talking about something wrong. I mean something going on that was wrong. I don't know for sure what it means. It all sounded kind of mysterious. . . ."

"Oh, no. Not this again." Hasty shook his head.

"Not what?"

"It's just that every time you get involved in something mysterious, I get in trouble. Last time I had to explain to my folks how I got mixed up with the snake lady and those carnival people. Now you've got me messing with a talking pinball machine. How am I going to tell my mom and dad about a talking pinball machine?"

Pitch looked at the pinball machine. "I don't think it's anything like that. Only . . ."

"Only what?" Hasty scratched his head.

"Only I wish I knew where that voice came from—that really chews at me."

3.

THE VOICE did not come again, and when they ran out of quarters they left the arcade and went down by the dam on the outskirts of town. There was an old abandoned power plant where the water ran through the spillway, and it was a good place to prowl around. It was also a good place to find things that the current brought down the river.

Once Pitch and Hasty had found a small boat, a sailing dinghy that had broken loose somewhere upstream. Somehow it had gotten through the spillway, a kind of concrete trough next to the dam, without breaking. It was a beautiful little red boat, just big enough for the two of them, and they had decided to ride in it for a while and the current took them and that was how they got involved with the snake lady and the carnival.

Another time they had found a sack full of dolls floating and that took them into the doll mystery where Hasty got mad because he had to wear a wig. So they often came down to the spillway to check things out.

Also, it was a good location for Pitch to do heavy thinking. To the left of the spillway was a concrete buttress that stuck out into the current and Pitch would find himself sitting on the end of the buttress with the water roaring around him when he wanted to think.

The two boys rumbled around a bit, looking through the rocks.

Hasty found some good driftwood and wanted to take it home. One piece was in the shape of an only slightly small Tyrannosaurus Rex. But his mother had put the clamps down on his bringing home more driftwood. He had filled his room with it, had pieces stuck in four or five other rooms, and had finally left a piece across the entryway to the house without telling his father, who made a shallow dent in the front door with his head when he tripped in the dark, and wanted to make a shallow dent in Hasty before the headache wore off and he settled down.

Hasty sadly put the prehistoric wooden animal on a rock, positioned it to seem as if it was going to spring, and turned to see Pitch sitting out on the end of the buttress, holding his knees and staring down into the white water.

Hasty worked down the concrete and sat next to his friend. For a moment he said nothing. There was something about the water, the noise of the water, that made him quiet. Then he leaned close to Pitch's ear and yelled.

"What's the matter?"

Pitch shook his head. "I don't know."

Hasty thought another moment. "It was that voice, wasn't it?"

Pitch looked at Hasty, then back to the water. He nodded. "Yes."

Hasty watched the water pour over the dam for a minute. "We're going to go back, aren't we?"

Pitch nodded. "Yes."

Again Hasty thought a minute. "This is one of those things where you won't stop until you find out about it, isn't it?"

Another nod. "Yes."

Hasty smiled. "Then I've got a question."

"What?"

"How come we're sitting out here?"

Pitch answered the smile with one of his own and stood. There was plenty of room on top of the concrete, but when he stood he weaved and seemed to teeter, and Hasty grabbed his T-shirt.

"Don't fall in. I wouldn't be able to catch you for two miles." He motioned down at the current. "It really whips by here. . . ."

But Pitch was scrambling back up the ramp and heading for his bicycle. "Come on. We're going back to the arcade."

He was pedaling before he finished speaking, and Hasty had to jump to keep up.

4.

OLD PETEY sold them some game tokens and they went straight to the pinball machine. An adult was playing it, a tall, thin man with a leather jacket all covered with metal studs. On the back of the jacket was a drawing of a skull with fangs dripping blood. Oh good, Pitch thought. I needed this. He stood on one side and Hasty stood on the other. The man was an expert and had two free games waiting on the counter.

Pitch watched the man play three balls and then coughed. "Been playing the machine long?"

The man looked at him, then at Hasty, then back at Pitch. "No. Why? You in a hurry?"

Pitch shook his head. Hasty moved off for the Total Devastator game. He was good at avoiding trouble. Mostly. Pitch shrugged. "I was playing it before and it acted kind of weird. I just wondered if it was acting normal now."

"What do you mean, weird? How was it acting?"

Pitch coughed again. "Well. Voices."

"Voices?"

"Yeah. Kind of mumbling voices. You hear anything like that?"

"Are you sure your elevator goes all the way to the top floor?"

Pitch smiled. "I guess you didn't hear any voices."

"Listen, kid, I don't hear voices unless there are people making them, you got that? Now let me play my game here or I'll pinch your head."

Well, Pitch thought—guess I'll mosey on over to the Total Devastator area. The guy looked like he ate cars. He left the man and went to watch Hasty beat the machine.

The man in the leather jacket played off his two free games, and then two more that he paid for—Pitch was beginning to fidget and threw off Hasty's rhythm—before he walked out of the arcade.

Pitch went back to the Motocross pinball and dropped a token in. Lights came on, a glaring sign lit up and told him to "start your engines" in white letters, and the first ball popped up, ready to shoot. He released the plunger and fired it, played the ball as well as he could. Nothing. He played the next ball. Nothing. Then the next three and still no sound except for the normal machine sounds. Another quarter, another game, and still no voice.

So. Maybe he had imagined it. Maybe it was all a strange dream or something.

He stood with his hands on the flipper buttons and stared at the back of the pinball machine. No. The voice had been real. It had been the voice of a boy, or something like that. A funny-sounding voice. But it had been real. He was sure of it.

Maybe there was something in the back of the machine. A speaker or something. Or maybe in the wall. The problem was that the way the machines were pushed back against the wall it was impossible to see from the side if there was anything back in there. But if I get underneath, he thought, maybe I could see something.

Pitch looked around the arcade. Hasty was still working the Total Devastator game. Old Petey was sitting at the change booth, handing tokens to four kids who were standing so that their bodies blocked off Petey's vision a bit.

Pitch scrambled down and back under the machine. It was dark and dusty and smelled bad. He moved on all fours to the wall and tried to see up between the back of the machine and the wall.

It was too dark at first. But he shielded his eyes with his hands and after a few seconds his eyes got used to the darkness. Still, he could see nothing for a moment, and then he saw it. A faint line of raised metal bolted to the wall. It didn't make any sense. Why would there be a raised ridge of metal on the wall—and why would it speak to him?

Wait a minute. He closed out more light with his hands, mashed his head against the wall and squinted. There. He could see it better. It was a ventilator grate. He was looking at the edge of a ventilator grate bolted to the wall.

The voice had been coming out of a ventilator shaft.

"What are you doing down there?"

The voice boomed so loudly that he jumped and slammed his head up against the bottom of the machine, drilling his skull into a screw that stuck out, so hard the pain made his eyes cross.

"Get out of there now! No crawling under the machines. Can't you read the signs?" Petey was yelling from the coin booth, his bellow peeling the paint off the walls.

Pitch wriggled out backwards like a worm. "I dropped a quarter. . . ."

"No crawling under the machines," Petey repeated, and pointed to a sign on the wall. Rule Seven actually said it—There will be no crawling under the machines.

"I'm sorry." I wonder, Pitch thought, as Petey

went back to making change, how many kids crawl around under the machines. Probably dozens. I'll bet you could come in here sometimes and that's all they're doing, crawling around under the machines. It's a new kind of hobby. Machine crawling.

He gave a nod to Hasty, who was watching him, and went out of the arcade. Hasty caught up with him in the main entry hall that led to the other stores in the mall.

"What did you find?"

"A ventilator. The voice was coming out of a ventilator."

"So what comes next?"

Pitch opened the door to the hallway that went to the restrooms. It was next door to the arcade. "Simple. We've got to find out where the ventilator goes."

"Got to?" Hasty asked, following him through the door. "Why is it always 'got to'?"

But Pitch was already too far ahead to hear him.

5.

NEXT TO the video arcade was a door that led to a hallway. On the other side of the hall was the T-shirt store, where you could get anything you wanted printed on a T-shirt. The hallway ran back to two restrooms, and at the very end, a door that led to the left, which Pitch and Hasty had never tried.

Pitch went first into the bathroom, looked up at the ceiling and nodded when he saw a ventilator opening about two feet square, high up in the corner of the wall above the sinks. He and Hasty were both looking up at the ventilator when a man came in to use the bathroom. The man saw them, walked over to them and looked up.

"What's up there?"

Hasty shrugged. "A ventilator."

"But what's in it?"

"Nothing. Air, I guess."

"Then why are you looking up at it?"

Hasty looked at the man, then shrugged again. "I don't really know. . . ."

"Crazy kids." The man shook his head and went into one of the stalls.

Pitch studied the ventilator for a couple more seconds, then sighed. "I don't think it's the right location."

He went out of the bathroom and paced the number of steps back to the door leading into the mall opening. Then he went through the door, back to the arcade and paced the steps from the arcade opening back to the pinball. He shook his head, standing by the rack of pay phones. "No. It can't be that vent. They aren't lined up at all."

Hasty was used to his friend's strange mannerisms. But now and then he got frustrated when he couldn't quite figure out what Pitch was doing. Which was most of the time. "Do you mind telling me what you're talking about?"

"The voice was kind of soft. Or had soft edges or something. It just teases me because I know I've heard that voice, or that kind of voice before but I can't think of where. It's just that whoever was talking, I don't think they were speaking all that loud."

"And that means the voice didn't come from the bathroom vent?"

Pitch nodded. "It doesn't line up with the pinball machine on the other side of the wall. I think the voice had to come in a straight line. If it went around too many corners we—I mean I wouldn't have heard it."

Hasty got a sudden itch in the back of his knee and reached down to scratch it. When he straightened up Pitch was gone, that fast, and he saw the door to the hallway swinging or he wouldn't have known where to go.

He hurried to catch up. It seemed like he was always hurrying to catch up. Pitch was past the restrooms and to the door at the end of the hall. He tried the knob and it was locked. Close to the door Hasty could see a small brown sign that read, VENTI-LATION ACCESS.

"We've got to get in there." Pitch twisted the knob again.

"But it's locked."

Pitch rubbed his hair. It was red-brown and wiry. "If we can't find out where the voice came from we can't do anything about it. And if we can't trace the ventilator pipe back we can't find where the voice came from. So we've got to get in there, right?"

Hasty nodded. "What scares me is when you start

to make sense to me." He thought a moment. "Listen, are you sure it's all that important? I mean all you heard was somebody saying something was wrong—is it all that big a deal?"

Pitch looked at Hasty and said nothing.

Hasty nodded. "Right. It's a mystery. I almost forgot."

"So we've got to get into that room," Pitch said. Then his face brightened and he snapped his fingers. "Or get inside the ventilating system."

Hasty stared at him. "You mean inside the pipes and stuff?"

"Sure. We're small enough. That grate in the bathroom was big enough to climb up into. All we have to do is get inside there and crawl around until we figure out where the sound came from. . . ."

"That's crazy."

But Pitch was gone. He ran out to his bike and brought in the small tool kit he carried in the seat bag. "Come on and stand guard."

"I don't know . . ." Hasty started. But of course he followed.

At the restroom, Pitch stopped just inside the door, bent down, and looked under the stalls. The room was empty. He went to the sinks and scrambled up, putting the open tool packet on the shelf below the mirrors. "Good. It's just plain screws, four of them. You stand outside the door and cough loud if somebody comes. I'll call you when I'm ready."

"I don't know . . ." Hasty said, but he went outside the door and watched. It seems like that's all I say, he thought, leaning against the wall near the door. I don't know. A woman came into the hallway, pulling a small boy along by one hand, but she dragged him into the ladies' restroom, and nobody else came.

"All right," Pitch hissed through the door. "Come on."

Hasty went back inside the bathroom and saw Pitch already up in the ventilator, backed in, holding the grate with one hand and waving for him to come with the other. "Hurry up. Before somebody comes."

I don't know, Hasty thought. But this time he didn't say it. Things were happening too fast for talking. He pulled himself up on the sink, slithered into the ventilator opening and wriggled past Pitch. It was a tight fit, but they could just get past each other. "Wait a minute," Pitch whispered. He pulled the grate back into place, where it slid into its mounting brackets snugly enough to hold.

"We made it!" Pitch giggled. "I thought it would be harder."

For a moment there was silence, broken only by the hum of a fan in some far-off place. There were also strange clunks and rattles that must have come from machinery of some kind. Pitch scrabbled back around in the tiny shaft until he was facing forward, then wormed past Hasty to take the lead. "Let's go."

With the grate back in place much of the light was blocked off, so the shaft was almost dark. And what little light did come through, their bodies pretty well stopped. Pitch quickly disappeared into the darkness on his hands and knees but Hasty held back.

"Pitch?" he whispered. The ventilator shaft seemed as dark as the inside of an old tennis shoe. In the back of a closed closet with a burned-out bulb. In a haunted house. In the basement. He tried it louder. "Pitch?"

But there was no answer. He waited two more beats of his heart and then started crawling forward at a half lope to catch up.

"I feel," he said to himself, half aloud, trying to peer ahead into the darkness, "like I'm about to be swallowed by something."

6.

HASTY DIDN'T catch Pitch right away. After what seemed like three or four days of slithering in the black tube, but was probably only two minutes, Hasty found himself at an intersection where one shaft went straight ahead, one went left and another right. There was no indication of which way Pitch had gone. Hasty felt right, then left, then straight, groping with his fingers, looking for some clue. Oh great, he thought. Just great.

"Pitch!" he whispered as loudly as he could without actually yelling. Or screaming, which is what he wanted to do. Man, he thought, this is the very worst. Dragging me into the darkest, tightest place in the world just because some silly voice came out of a pinball machine. He'd try one more time and if he didn't get an answer he'd turn around and go back. "Pit . . . ahhhhrrg!"

Right in the middle of the word something grabbed at his face, his whole face and he screamed. He couldn't help it.

"Quiet!" Pitch hissed. "It's just me. I came back for you. Now come on. And for pete's sake, keep up. You want to get lost?" He turned and was gone again before Hasty could answer.

Like he knows where we are, Hasty thought—sure. Like I know where we are. We're being swallowed by a building, that's where we are. But this time he didn't wait and was fast on Pitch's heels, actually touching the back of Pitch's shoe with his hand as he crawled. His mind was full of things that lived in dark places. Snakes, spiders, rats as big as house cats, centipedes that crawled on your skin and up your nose when you lay dead . . . he shook his head. No, he thought—I do not want to get lost.

Their eyes were becoming used to the darkness now and the boys could almost but not quite see things. Pitch stopped and turned, and if he looked to the side of Hasty's head he could just make out his friend's face. He continued crawling and in a few moments came to another intersection.

"I think this shaft to the left is the one that leads to the grate in back of the pinball machine," Pitch said. Straight ahead the noise seemed to be louder, the hum and rattle of machinery. "Straight must be to the equipment room. We have to go to the right."

He moved around the corner and set off, Hasty following. Now they went a long ways and it became truly thick, black dark, so that they couldn't see even faint outlines. What's more it seemed to be getting dusty, and Hasty twice sneezed so hard it brought him to a stop and he nearly lost contact with Pitch.

At length they came to a Y intersection, with two branches that went off at angles. Pitch stopped. "It could be either one."

Hasty opened his eyes wider but still couldn't see Pitch. "I'm not having fun."

Pitch laughed. "Come on—it's not that bad."

"Where do you figure we are?"

"It's pretty hard to measure. I think we're moving through the roof in the shaft and maybe we're halfway across the mall." Pitch sighed. "I'm pretty sure the voice must have come from one of these shafts— but which one?"

"Well let's try one of them—anything is better than sitting here." Hasty was having mental images of centipedes and rats as big as house cats again. It was so dark.

"Okay. We'll go to the right." Pitch set off again. Hasty gained on him rapidly. He had worked out a kind of sideways shuffle—like a crab—that kept him moving forward at a fast clip, and after a bit he got almost a cocky feeling about it. He could hang back a bit and easily catch up, with a couple of sideways scrabbles. I'm a tunnel crab, he thought, moving through the tunnel. Faster than night animals I move through the tunnel, sliding along sideways—

"What the . . . ?" With a silent ooomph he ran up against Pitch and slammed into his back. "What's the matter?"

"Shhh!" Pitch reached a hand around and put it over Hasty's mouth. Hasty could see now that they were at another grate. Light filtered through and he could easily see Pitch's eyes, which were wide and white.

He pushed Pitch's hand away from his mouth, whispered softly. "Where are we?"

"Turn around. Go back."

"What's the matter? Where are we?"

"Go back. We're at Kearney's dress shop. Over the dressing room."

"What do you see?"

"It's Miss Olsen."

"You mean our teacher last year? You mean old Hatchet Olsen?" Miss Olsen had the reputation of being the toughest, meanest teacher in school. She didn't take prisoners. Once she had drawn two circles on the blackboard and made Hasty stand with his hands in the circles for a whole period, just for a misunderstanding about a rubber band and a spitball and the back of Stevey Dunning's head. Hasty tried to get around him. "Let me see. . . ."

"No. Turn around." Pitch pushed Hasty back and kept pushing until they were well away from the grate. Then Hasty, who was ahead, heard a small giggle.

"What's so funny?"

"Oh, nothing . . ."

"Come on."

"Well. It's just that Miss Olsen isn't real."

"What do you mean?"

Pitch giggled again. "There's a lot of stuff underneath that isn't Miss Olsen. That's all I'll say." He moved ahead of Hasty again and soon they were back at the Y.

"It must have been the other way." Pitch started to the right and this time they hadn't gone far when he stopped and Hasty again saw light around him from another grate. Pitch put his eye to one of the slotted grate openings and studied what lay on the other side. "Now I know what it was . . ." he said, nearly to himself.

"What is it?" Hasty tried to see around him but couldn't get to the grate. "What's down there?"

"It's the pet store," Pitch said. "Devin's pet store. The grate is in the back room. And now I know what the voice was—I knew it was something I had heard before. I just couldn't think of it. But now that I see where it came from I know it."

"Who was it?"

"Not who—what."

"What do you mean?"

"The voice was a parrot."

"A parrot?"

"A parrot. You know, like a bird. A parrot. The voice had that parrot sound."

Hasty stared at him in the half light through the grate. "You mean I'm in here with centipedes and rats as big as house cats because a parrot said something was wrong?"

"Centipedes? Rats? What are you talking about?" Pitch turned and started back toward the bathroom grate, squeezing past Hasty. "There aren't any rats or centipedes in here." And he was gone in the darkness.

Hasty, the tunnel crab, shuffled to catch up.

"A parrot," he snorted, the dust whistling out of his nose. "What does a parrot know?"

7.

TO MAKE matters worse the bathroom was full. Pitch stopped at the grate and held his hand back to stop Hasty. They could hear water running in the sink beneath the grate. Pitch put his eye to the grate opening and saw four men.

The water ran.

Hasty started to squirm. "Are they gone yet?" He whispered into Pitch's ear.

Pitch shook his head. "No. More came in. We have to wait."

The water ran.

Hasty squirmed more. "Aren't they gone yet?"

Pitch looked. Shook his head. "They're still there. Two left."

The water ran.

"I can't wait." Hasty pushed. "I can't wait any-more. . . ."

Pitch held him back. "There are two men down there."

The water ran.

"I DON'T CARE. I GOTTA GO. NOW!" Hasty yelled and knocked the grate loose, jumped down to the sink and ran into a stall.

The men standing at the sink looked up in stunned amazement as the two boys piled out of the corner ventilator near the ceiling. They were too surprised to move. Pitch turned, still standing on the sink, picked up the grate from the sink where it had fallen and put it back in the hole. He took the screws out of one pocket and his small bike tool case out of another and screwed the grate to the wall mounts without looking around, whistling through his teeth.

All this time the men stared at him in silence. Hasty came out of the stall just as Pitch finished and jumped down from the sink. He put the tool packet back in his pocket and dusted his hands. He smiled, looked up at the two men who were still silent.

"Shortcut," Pitch said. "Best way to get across the mall. . . ."

And they walked out the door. As soon as they were in the hall they took off running until they cleared the door into the main part of the mall, then Pitch stopped. He was laughing.

"Shortcut?" Hasty giggled, leaning against the wall to catch his breath. "How did you come up with that?"

"It was the first thing to come to my mind." He stopped laughing suddenly and looked for a clock. "What time is it?"

Hasty had a watch. It was digital but sometimes it skipped an hour. "It's either three or four. I think it might be three. You know, we were only in the shaft for fifteen minutes. It seemed like a week." He shook his head. "Like my whole life. Why did you want to know the time?"

"I just wondered if we had time to check out the pet store before the library closes." He frowned. "I think the library closes at five o'clock today."

"What are you going to check out at the pet store and the library?"

"Why, parrots," Pitch said, "what else?" He trotted off in the direction of the pet store.

"What else?" Hasty repeated, following along, as he seemed to be always following. "Silly question."

Devin's pet store was located in the back of the mall. They trotted past the waterbed store, a large discount center and finally saw the pet store. Hasty marveled at how far they had come through the ceiling in the ventilator shaft. Crawling over all these people without being seen.

Devin's was laid out simply. The front of the store

was a glass window filled with paper signs and painted messages about things on sale.

GUPPIES.

KITTENS.

PUPPIES.

The boys looked in the window before going in. To the right was the entrance door that led directly to a glass counter full of all the odds and ends of materials used for taking care of pets. Flea powder, parakeet food, collars, and leashes. On the end of the counter was a cash register. Next to the counter was an open floor area with a free-standing set of shelves holding more pet materials. All around the walls were cages and glass boxes and aquariums full of puppies and kittens, birds, and fish, in that order. One set of glass cases had snakes coiled on pieces of dry driftwood—they looked like boa constrictors or pythons and were not moving—and another an iguana lizard. It was also completely still—it looked stuffed. In the rear left corner of the pet store was a door leading to the back.

"Let's go in." Pitch swung the door open and walked inside. As soon as they entered, a bell rang and four cocker spaniel puppies in cages to the rear started yapping at them, whining and pushing their noses against the cages, flicking their tongues out.

"They're so cute," Hasty said. "I wish I could have

one." His parents wouldn't allow any pets because his little sister, Alice, was—as he put it—completely allergic to anything there was in the world. Period. "I can't even have a goldfish. I think she's allergic to water or something."

"I don't see any parrots." Pitch studied the room. There was nobody there, but as they looked around at the cages and cases the back doorway opened and a man came through. He was tall, with rounded shoulders and dark hair cut short and combed back tightly so that it came from a point high in the middle of his forehead. His eyes were brown and lifted a bit at the outer corners.

He looks, Pitch thought, like the devil.

The man smiled—his teeth uneven but white, which somehow made him look still more like a devil—and stopped in front of them. "I was in the back room, doing something. Can I help you?"

Hasty shook his head. "Just looking. Just looking around, you know. Just looking at things. Just looking."

Pitch kicked his leg from the side to shut him up. What a time for Hasty to get motormouth. He looked up at the man, who seemed to tower over them. "We've been by here lots of times and never come in. We just thought we'd see what you have."

"Just looking," Hasty put in again. "Not for anything particular, you know. Just kind of browsing. Looking."

"Well, it's a pet store." The man studied them carefully. "We sell pets and pet supplies. Go ahead, look around."

Pitch swung his eyes around the room as if seeing the shelves for the first time. "I don't see any parrots. Do you sell them?"

"Parrots?" The man raised his eyebrow and shook his head. "Nope. They are so rare we don't stock them. In fact you can't even special order them. We lean more toward canaries and parakeets. If you'd want a good parakeet I could help you out. But no parrots."

"I was kind of looking for something that talks. Talks more like a person."

"Parakeets can be trained to talk. You take one home and you can have it talking in two or three weeks. Just work with it."

"Do you have any here that talk already?" Pitch waved his arm around in a circle. "You know, here in the store or maybe in the back room?"

The pet store owner again shook his head. "No . . . there's nothing in the back room but shipping crates and boxes. We keep everything live out front where it can be seen by our customers."

"I see. . . ."

"Why would you ask about the back room?" The store owner raised his eyebrows again and looked even more like a devil. Pitch could hear Hasty's breath stop for a second next to him.

"No reason," Pitch said, shrugging. "I just thought there might be some animals back there."

"Well, there aren't."

"Oh, well, then . . ."

For a moment they stood there, the two boys in front of the man, a moment that seemed to grow until it became uncomfortable. Finally the man broke the silence. "If there isn't anything else . . ."

"We have to get going," Hasty said, pulling at Pitch's T-shirt. "Got to get home, don't we? We'd better head on down the road, don't you think?"

Pitch allowed himself to be pulled from the store back into the mall until they were around the corner. The store owner watched them until they were out of sight.

"I knew it," Pitch said when they got in front of the drugstore and couldn't be seen. "Did you see that? Did you hear that? That guy was lying through his teeth."

Hasty shuddered. "As far as I'm concerned, if he wants to lie through them, he can. Let's go do something more fun. Like smash our thumbs with a hammer. I don't think we should have anything to do with him. He makes my life pass in front of my eyes."

"Well, you can go play if you want. I tell you there's something funny going on here and I'm not done with it yet. I'm not even close to done with it."

Hasty sighed. "That's the exact same thing you said when we got mixed up with the dolls and I had to wear the wig. I was afraid this was going to happen."

But as usual Pitch was gone before he got the words out and Hasty had to hurry to catch up.

"DID YOU ever feel like we live two different lives?" Hasty pulled his bike up next to Pitch at the red light on Main Street and stopped with one foot down. It was two more blocks to the library and Pitch had set a fast-paced cadence to his pedaling that had both boys sweating. The library was due to close in thirty minutes, and Pitch was worried that they'd get caught in traffic and be late.

"What do you mean?" Pitch took deep breaths until he caught up to himself. It was a hot evening with heavy traffic, and his legs ached pleasantly from the work. "What two lives?"

"Well, like I've got to be home at five-thirty with my family and we'll sit down and eat dinner and watch television and then I'll go to bed and my folks will say good night. . . ."

"So?" Pitch watched the light but it was still red. Cars streamed past.

"So if I told them that we heard a parrot say something was wrong and then we crawled through the ventilating system of Harrington's Mall or saw Miss Olsen—that is you saw Miss Olsen—in a dressing room or that we found the devil in a pet store . . . well, they'd think I was whacky. It's like that part of my life is a whole other life."

The light for the cars went to yellow and Pitch moved his pedal to get ready. "I see what you mean. But I think it's best not to think about it. Right now we've got to get to the library."

As soon as the light went green they kicked out and crossed Main to get to the library parking lot. Once there they locked their bikes and Pitch trotted up the steps, almost running. He seemed to be almost always almost running.

Outside, the library building appeared to be very old. It had a high stone entrance with carved granite urns on either side of the door. It was surrounded by modern tall buildings that made it look even older and more tired.

But that was only the outside. The inside had been remodeled so that it was ultra-modern and had the most up-to-date computer and reference systems. At the front was an information desk. The woman in charge of the desk was named Mary Anne Jamison and she knew Pitch and Hasty on sight.

"Hello," she greeted them. "What is it this time?"

"Parrots." Pitch leaned on the desk. "We need to know everything there is to know about parrots."

Ms. Jamison smiled. "Last time it was dolls, and the time before that circuses. What's so important about parrots?"

Pitch looked at Hasty and shrugged. "We just got . . . curious. Some things happened to make us think of parrots and we realized we didn't know anything about them. So here we are—which way to the parrots?"

Ms. Jamison left the information desk, went to the computer console located just to the rear, and punched in the general reference program, requesting any and all information available on parrots. The screen showed nothing for a moment, then it splashed green with line after line of books and titles of articles until it was covered with them. Ms. Jamison scrolled it and the list went on and on.

"That's all on parrots?" Hasty said. "Just on parrots?"

"Quite a bit, isn't it?" She laughed. "Maybe you'd just like to see some general information about them. Here's a book titled *The World of Parrots*. How about that?"

"It would be a good place to start." Pitch nodded. "Where is it?"

Ms. Jamison directed them to the right shelf and went to help somebody at the information desk.

"We'll have to check it out," Pitch said, finding the shelf and pulling a large book down. It had a color picture of a parrot on the cover. "It's too big to look at here in only twenty minutes."

"Maybe we should get more," Hasty said. "I could take a book home too—we could get twice as much done."

"Good idea." Pitch went both ways on the shelf and finally found another book that seemed promising. *Exotic Birds* was the title, but there was a picture of another kind of parrot on the cover and he saw more pictures of parrots inside. He handed it to Hasty and they went to the checkout desk, checked the books against Pitch's card—Hasty had forgotten his—and went back outside.

"I have just time to get home," Hasty said. "My folks will get upset if I'm late." He put his book under the spring hook on his rear wheel rack and swung a leg over. "Call me later."

Pitch watched him ride away, then on second thought went back into the library. He was also supposed to be in by five-thirty but his mom and dad were loose about it and didn't care if he was a few minutes late.

Ms. Jamison smiled when she saw Pitch again. "Not enough for you?"

Pitch nodded. "That's sort of it. I just want to know everything I can know. I thought if I maybe had another book or two or something . . . I don't know what. I just wanted to know more."

"About parrots?" Ms. Jamison asked. "What's so important about parrots?"

Pitch smiled. "That's what Hasty wants to know. The truth is I'm not sure. Something strange happened and I think it's all about parrots and I just need to know. I guess that's all. It's not important, really, but it is, too. Does that make any sense?"

She shook her head. "Not much. But if you want to know something, anything, the library is the place to come. And it's free. How about if you tell me what you need to know about parrots. What part about parrots is so important?"

"Well . . . I guess I need to know if there's something that can be wrong about them."

"Wrong about parrots?" She frowned. "You mean like diseases?"

Pitch shook his head. "No. Not that way. I mean maybe illegal. Can something be done wrong with parrots?"

"I see. I see." Ms. Jamison stood. "I think the best thing to do is go through past newspaper stories and magazine articles. We have them all on film in our film record. But it will take some time and we're about to close. . . ." She raised one eyebrow in a question.

Pitch took the hint. "I'll come back in the morning and bring Hasty." And once more he turned and left the library. But speaking the second time to Ms. Jamison had triggered his thinking.

The library had started his brain working along a certain path and he rode slowly and quietly home, mentally chewing on what he had started:

Something illegal with parrots.

9.

THE PHONE rang at nine o'clock exactly and Pitch ran for it. He also had a sister, named Amanda, who was fourteen and got about four hundred phone calls a day, and she usually beat him to the phone, but this time he made it with almost four inches to spare. He snatched the receiver with one hand clawed, bouncing off the wall with his left shoulder and dropping neatly into the chair by the phone.

"Hello."

"It's me," Hasty said—he never said who it was exactly, only, it's me. "I think I have it."

"Have what?"

"The answer to what's going on with the parrots."

"Your book must have been better than mine," Pitch said, sighing. He had read for two hours and so far knew only that most parrots came from South

America, that they came in many different colors and sizes and shapes, that they could be taught to talk—along with parakeets, crows, ravens and several other birds—and that they were fairly clean. Or at least seemed to be. "What's going on with the parrots?

"Buried treasure."

"What?"

"I know, I know. I thought it was stupid at first too, but when you hear what I found it might change your mind."

"What did you find?"

"The thing is this book about exotic birds is really interesting. Man, I didn't know there were that many weird birds in the world. Did you know that there's a bird in the mountains in Colorado that jumps off of little rocks and flies underwater . . . ?"

"No. I did not know there's a bird in Colorado that jumps off of little rocks and flies underwater. And I also do not see what that has to do with parrots."

"Oh. Nothing. I just got into the book and started to have fun. But in the part about parrots I found out two things. One is that they're pretty valuable, but even more important is that this guy says parrots live to be really old."

"How old?"

"A hundred."

"You mean a hundred years?"

"Yeah. And some get even older. They can get to a hundred and twenty or thirty years old."

"Wow."

"Yeah. So I started doing some thinking. Parrots almost always went with pirates, right?"

"Well . . ."

"Really. You never see a picture of a pirate without a parrot around somewhere. Usually on his shoulder. And pirates always had buried treasure, right?"

"Well . . ."

"So I was thinking what if a parrot who used to belong to a pirate is in the back of the pet store. From a real pirate from way back when, maybe a hundred and twenty years ago, and this parrot actually knew the location of a buried treasure. Had heard the pirate describe how to get to it. You know, like twenty steps from the old haunted tree or something like that. So they've got this parrot held, like you know, hostage back there."

"Well . . ."

"Just a minute." Hasty turned away from the phone and spoke to his parents but Pitch could hear it. "I'll be right there. This is a really important call. Just start to run the water and I'll be right there."

He turned back to the phone. "I've got to take a bath and get ready for bed. Do you believe it? I thought that now that I was a year older they'd let me stay up a little later—but no. Bath and bed by ten-thirty at the latest. Anyway, think about what I said, all right? It could be there's a parrot being held against his will back there and he might be the key to a buried treasure."

"Or maybe not," Pitch said, smiling. Sometimes Hasty really came off the wall with things. It was like his brain was set on high speed and when a simple idea hit it the machinery just took off on it. They said goodbye and hung up and Pitch headed for his own bath. It was Friday and they both got nailed on Friday night. Sometime during the week as well. But for sure on Friday night.

Which made no sense to Pitch. He'd get dirty all over again on Saturday, dirty with weekend dirt and everybody knew weekend dirt was worse than during-the-week dirt. Pitch asked his mom once why she insisted on Friday baths and she said it was because her mom had given her Friday baths and that made it the night to get a bath. And that was parent logic.

He took his bath and went to bed, propped up squeaky clean with the parrot book on his lap. Maybe, he thought, I missed something. But as he read he became drowsy and learned nothing more except that parrots were exceptionally intelligent—much more intelligent than other birds—and he fell asleep, finally, thinking of a parrot sitting on a perch with glasses on, reading a book about people that said people were fairly smart and knew where buried treasure could be found.

It made for strange dreams.

10.

"IT CAME to me this morning when I woke up," Pitch said. "It was something you said you'd read."

The two boys were waiting at the front door to the library on Saturday morning. They had arrived almost fifteen minutes early and the front doors were still locked.

"So you think it might be buried treasure?" Hasty smiled. "You never do what I think. Maybe this is a first or something. . . ."

Pitch held up his hand. The morning sun was coming between the buildings and hitting his eyes, and he squinted with his right eye, which made him look like he was winking. "Not exactly. It was the other thing you said last night. About parrots being expensive. It must have stuck in my thoughts and my brain worked on it all night while I slept—in between the dreams."

Hasty watched a hot dog cart set up across the street on a corner. He loved hot dogs. Just plain. No mustard or butter on the bun. No catsup. Nothing but the hot dog and a bun. With the bun dry. "You got any money? I left home with nothing. I wonder how much the hot dogs are?"

"It was that bit about the parrots being worth a lot. I started to think about if they were worth a lot of money there might be people who steal them or something. . . ."

He stopped as the library doors were unlocked. Ms. Jamison was there. "Good morning. I see you're ready to go bright and early."

Pitch nodded. "We're learning. But we need more. Can you help us with the articles and stuff?"

She led them to the computer console. "It's really simple. You name the subject, which is parrots, and we look at the listing for parrots. It will show all the articles and newspaper stories about parrots for the period requested. Let's say you want everything for the last year on parrots. You just order it up and the computer tells you which microfilm for each one. Excuse me, there's someone at the desk." She left them and went to the desk by the door to help a man who looked lost.

Pitch and Hasty studied the titles on the screen.

" 'Teaching Parrots to Talk,' " Pitch read aloud. " 'Parrot Diseases,' 'Treating Parrot Bite Wounds,' 'Parrot Mange,' 'Parrot Moulting.' " He whistled. "Man, it sounds like parrots are a lot of messy work, doesn't it?"

Hasty nodded. "Also kind of painful . . ."

"There's more. It's kind of endless. Wait, here's what I've been looking for." He pushed the arrow to scroll the screen until the title he wanted was in the middle. " 'Police Investigate Parrot Smuggling.' I knew it—knew there had to be something going on with them because they were worth money, and there it is."

"There what is?" Ms. Jamison came up in back of them. "Did you find what you were looking for?"

Pitch nodded. "Could we see this one please?" He put his finger on the smuggling headline.

"Of course." She led them over to the microfilm machine. "We'll just feed in the right roll numbered on the screen and start scanning the articles until we get it." She began sliding the articles through the film viewer, passing them so rapidly that Pitch and Hasty could not read them. "Just a blur, isn't it? You get better with practice. I'm just spot reading bits as they go through until I get to the right one. Here. Here's the one you wanted."

She stopped suddenly, then backed it up. " 'Police Investigate Parrot Smuggling.' It was an article in the center section of the newspaper in October last year. Oh, I have to go again." She rose and went once more to the desk to help someone.

Pitch and Hasty read slowly.

"There were rumors of a major exotic bird smuggling ring somewhere in the state and that set off a police investigation," Pitch said, condensing the article. "They didn't find anything solid because they couldn't find the center. Twice they found crates of birds but didn't catch any people. Wow—it says here that some parrots are worth close to ten thousand dollars. Each."

They were silent for a moment, thinking of a bird worth that much.

"It's just a pretty chicken that can talk, right?" Hasty said, leaning back in the library chair. "What makes a parrot worth ten thousand dollars?"

Pitch read on. "It says that they're really becoming rare. Smugglers trap them in South America and smuggle them out into other countries where rich collectors buy them. They bring so much money because they're so scarce. Some of them are endangered species. Hmmm. It says here that some falcons are the same. That they bring thousands of dollars in the underground bird market because some of them are almost as rare as certain parrots."

Pitch leaned back in his chair and looked at the ceiling. Ms. Jamison was still at the front desk.

"You're doing it again, aren't you?" Hasty said.

"Doing what?"

"Thinking."

"Yes. I was thinking that things are right where they were before. It could be nothing is happening in that pet store—could be. Or it could be there is something wrong happening, like the parrot said. Right now it could go either way. The thing is I think they are smuggling birds, just like the police suspected before, but I don't know it for sure."

"We could go to the police," Hasty said, hopefully. "Turn it all over to them."

Pitch nodded. "We could. Except that right now there isn't anything to turn over to them. What would you do if you were a policeman and two kids came up to you and told you a parrot said something was wrong?"

"I see what you mean."

"There's only one thing to do," Pitch said, standing. "We have to go back to the mall and do a stakeout on the pet store. We have to know for certain what they're up to."

"I was afraid you'd say that."

11.

"ARE YOU sure we're doing the right thing?" Hasty asked.

"Be quiet now. We have to stay as quiet as possible," Pitch answered him. "The essence of a good stakeout is silence."

The boys were again crawling in the ventilator shaft. They had entered once more through the restroom near the video arcade. The restroom had been empty and they slipped easily up into the system, sliding the grate back into place.

Knowing which way to move made their progress much faster, and Hasty scuttled along while he spoke. "Well, this isn't a real stakeout, is it? Whoever heard of a stakeout where both the cops have to be home by five-thirty or they get grounded?"

57

"Just the same, we'll do it right. So be quiet."

At the Y they took the left turn and were soon at the grate overlooking the back room at the pet shop. Pitch motioned Hasty to hold back a bit and moved as silently as possible until he had one eye against a slot of the grate opening. He moved sideways to make room for Hasty.

The room below them was a typical storage room in the back of a store. There was a metal door to the left, going outside to the rear parking lot of the mall. There were no windows. To the right was the door leading to the front of the store. The walls were covered with shelves and on all the shelves were boxes and wrapped packages. In the middle of the room was a large crate with a ventilation hatch cover on top. The side of the crate was open and it seemed to hold cages loosely propped on one another. The cages were empty.

"That's strange," Pitch whispered. "It's almost as if they were waiting for something to come, isn't it?"

Hasty started to answer but the door to the front of the store opened suddenly and the owner came into the back room. Hasty's tongue stuck to the roof of his mouth.

The man pushed the large empty crate slightly to the side, then stepped to the back door and unlocked it, looked out, swore, and slammed the door. He went back to the front of the store.

A half hour passed, with Hasty fighting sneezes, and the owner came into the rear of the store again and jerked the door open. This time two burly men wearing T-shirts came in and he relocked the door.

"Is everything ready?" one of the new men asked, his voice loud.

"Almost." The owner spoke quietly. "Keep your voice down—we don't want the whole world to know."

"So what's the big deal? We're just a shipping point. We bring them in and you crate them and we ship them out. There's nothing to worry about."

"That's easy for you to say," the owner whispered. "You don't have a store to lose if you get caught."

"Oh come on—we're just shipping a few birds. Relax." The man went to the back door. "Now get ready and I'll bring them in from the van. We have them in empty beer cases. That's how they shipped them up from South America. . . ."

"We're not shipping," the owner said. "We're smuggling them. And if we get caught it's the same as if we were smuggling diamonds. So don't tell me to relax."

But the man had gone outside. He propped the back door open with a box and the two men brought in several cardboard beer boxes with Spanish writing on the sides. The owner went back to the front of the store for a moment to deal with a customer and the other two stacked the beer boxes next to the large wooden crate.

"Too bad there isn't real beer in the cases, isn't it?" one of them said.

"Yeah. I'm thirsty. What say we go for a drink while Devin crates the birds?"

"Good idea."

The two of them left, locking the door behind them.

"See?" Pitch whispered. "They're smugglers. Just like I thought. We must have heard one of the birds from the last shipment."

"Now shouldn't we contact the police?" Hasty hissed. He kept looking back over his shoulder down the long, dark tube of the ventilator shaft. He knew nothing was there. But he couldn't help it. "Can't the police take it from here?"

"Shhhh." Pitch put a hand on his shoulder to silence him. The door to the store opened and the owner came in again. He mumbled some curse words about the other two leaving but set to work alone as if used to working without help.

Pitch and Hasty watched from the grate as he opened the first beer case and took out a small, handmade wooden cage. It was fashioned of thin bamboo strips tied with bark, as if done in some jungle village. Inside the cage was a beautifully colored toucan with a large beak. The owner reached expertly into the cage and removed the toucan—which kept snapping its beak at him—and put the bird carefully into one of the cages in the crate.

The next box held a parrot, then another parrot, and still another toucan. In all there were four parrots, six toucans, and some smaller dark birds that the boys couldn't recognize because they hadn't been in the library books they had studied.

When it was done the owner carefully put the side of the crate back on, tightening it in place with wood screws. Then he brushed his hands off and went back to the front of the store.

"Now we get the police," Hasty repeated. "Let's go."

But Pitch held back. "No. If the police come now they'll just get the crate and the store owner. They won't know where the crate is going and the smuggling ring will still be in operation."

"All right," Hasty said. "All right. I can live with that. I mean can't you live with that? I can live with that."

"We have to find the base point. It's probably somewhere else in the city—a bigger pet store, maybe. A special one."

Pitch had the tool case out. From the outside the

ventilator grate was held in place by four screws, the same as the bathroom grate, and the heads couldn't be reached from the inside. But the mounting screws were in turn tightened into four small brackets that were held by four more screws to the inside of the shaft and he had them out in less than a minute.

"What are you doing?" Hasty said.

"We have to find out where the crate is going."

"So we'll let the police ask them. . . ."

"No. They won't answer. The only way is to hide in the crate."

"Hide in the crate? Oh now wait—are you completely crazy?"

"Come on. There's no time to argue. We can get in through that hatch on top. Hurry."

Pitch pushed the grate out and slid down until his feet rested on a stack of boxes. He half-helped half-dragged the reluctant Hasty out after him, then put the grate back in place.

"But aren't parrots like, you know, pigeons?" Hasty whispered. "Don't they like, you know, stink?"

"No time to talk. Hurry. Hurry." Pitch held a finger to his lips and opened the plate on top of the wooden crate. He stood on one of the beer crates and stepped over and down inside the crate until he was on two of the cages. Hasty, too terrified to stay outside and get caught if the owner or the men suddenly returned, followed Pitch and the two of them were soon jammed tightly in with the parrots, who squawked a bit—one of them swore in Spanish—and settled down. Pitch reached up and lowered the ventilation hatch into place. It had a spring lock which clicked with finality when it locked.

"We made it," Pitch said, almost silently into Hasty's ear. "Now we just sit quietly and wait."

"I was right," Hasty whispered sadly.

"About what?"

"Parrots stink."

12.

THE BOYS needn't have hurried. They sat in silence for minutes that dragged like days and nothing seemed to happen. Some light filtered through the air holes in the side but it was very faint, and the birds slept as if it were night.

"I have to sneeze," Hasty suddenly whispered. "Big time sneeze."

"Don't."

"It's the smell."

"Don't."

He couldn't hold it and he sneezed, but he kept it contained. It sounded like somebody hit a water balloon with a hammer. "Weemph!"

More silence.

Maybe, Pitch thought to himself, maybe I made a mistake. There just hadn't been time to think things out. There was the crate and they had to know where it went and they moved. But maybe it was a mistake—he had private thoughts now that he hadn't had before, thoughts he didn't tell Hasty. Like what would they do when they got to where the crate was going? Mistake. Or as Hasty would say, big time mistake.

They heard the door to the store open, the owner walk past the crate, and then the door open to the outside.

"You got it ready?" The two men came in. "All set to go?"

"No thanks to you. . . ." The owner was clearly mad. "All you guys do is party all the time."

"We deliver the goods, don't we? Hold the door open while we load this in the van."

The crate jerked sideways a bit, then tipped up.

"Ummph. What did you put in this thing—turkeys? It weighs a ton."

"It's the beer," the owner said. "It makes you weak. Hurry up, get this thing out of here before somebody comes back looking for me."

The crate wavered and rose. Pitch and Hasty wedged their arms against the movement and felt a thump as the crate bounced on the metal floor of the van. Then it scraped as it was pushed forward and there was a clanging sound as the rear door of the van slammed shut.

There was a pause, some mumbling outside the

van the boys could not quite understand, and the two front doors of the van opened as the men got in. The doors slammed, the engine started, and with a series of jerks they began moving.

Pitch had been angled down with his elbow in Hasty's ear and he carefully moved to get it free. One of the parrots awakened and made a sound, but the noise of the engine drowned it out.

The men drove for a long time without speaking. Pitch could feel Hasty next to him, knew he wanted to talk, but they remained silent. Any noise now would blow it—even a contained sneeze.

I wonder, Pitch thought, how far it is to the next point—the base for the operation? Maybe in another town. Poor birds. Just ripped out of the jungle like this and slammed into a whole other world. It must be hard on them. He tried to rehearse what they would do. Perhaps the crate wouldn't be opened right away when it arrived, and they could somehow get out when nobody was looking. No, they wouldn't be that lucky.

They'd have to rely on surprise. The smugglers wouldn't figure on having two boys in the crate. As soon as they opened it Pitch and Hasty would have to blast out and run for a door. No, even before that. They'd have to force the crate. He'd have to whisper the idea to Hasty. There was a chance if they did it right—a chance that one of them at least would get away. . . .

Get away and bring the police. Finally. I should have done what Hasty said, he thought—should have gotten the police earlier. Turned it over to them.

"This gets farther every time we drive it," the man driving the van said.

"It's the traffic," the other one answered. "This is the worst time of the day for traffic out to the airport."

Airport! The word seared into Pitch's brain like a laser beam. Airport. He felt Hasty stiffen and hold his breath next to him like he'd been hit with a bat in the stomach. Airport, he thought, his brain turning to putty—airport, that's where they fly airplanes from.

"All I know is if we don't personally load these babies on the loading ramp at the plane by three-thirty, traffic or not, we don't get paid."

Big time, Pitch thought—big time mistake.

He felt/heard Hasty moan next to him.

Airport.

13.

THINGS WERE not going well.

The van stopped for a moment and there was a metallic rattling outside—the sound of gates being opened—then the van started moving again, drove only a short distance and stopped.

The men got out, slammed the side doors and opened the back door. Immediately the crate was filled with the deafening, roaring sounds of a busy airport. The thunder of jet engines seemed to be in every square corner of the world. Even the parrots awakened and started screeching.

Pitch couldn't think, couldn't make any part of his mind or body work. Hasty stiffened beside him. The crate was rudely jerked backward, out of the van, tumbling the boys onto each other and the cages of birds. It tipped this way and that and was slammed down on something that rumbled and moved beneath it, carrying it up at an angle.

"We're going up the luggage conveyor!" Hasty put his mouth to Pitch's ear and Pitch could still barely hear him. "Into the baggage compartment of the plane. I saw it once on a trip to my grandmother's house."

There was another bump as the crate dropped flat and was pushed by other luggage into a corner. More boxes and suitcases came in on top of the crate and in moments—still before either boy could think or act—there was a whooshing sound as the hatch was closed, and sudden almost-quiet.

"Hasty?"

"Ohhh . . ."

"Are you all right?"

"What a question. I think I'm upside down in a crate full of parrots that smell like pigeons in the belly of an airplane going where I don't know or even care to guess—and you ask if I'm all right?"

"We have to make a plan." Pitch squirmed around in the crate until he thought he was facing Hasty. The luggage compartment of the plane was completely dark and blocked out any chance of even a faint glow. It was totally dark, so that his eyes couldn't get used to it. "We have to be ready for what happens at the other end. . . ."

He stopped talking as the plane's engines began to roar louder and louder and they felt it start to move backward.

"We're moving!" Hasty almost yelled. "The plane is moving. We're going to take off, we're going to take off, we're going to take off. . . ."

The plane moved backward for another half a minute, then the engines roared still louder—inside the baggage compartment it was truly deafening—and it taxied forward. They could not speak, could not even yell to each other and be heard.

After a few more minutes the plane stopped. The engines died down a bit and Hasty leaned close to Pitch.

"Maybe they're going to turn around. Maybe they're not going to take off. . . ."

There was a sudden, thundering roar from the engines, a roar that filled the whole baggage compartment, and they were slammed against the side of the crate by the lunging of the plane as it shot forward down the runway.

"Noooooooooo. . . ."

Hasty yelled as the plane rolled faster and faster, the hammering of the cracks in the runway coming up through the wheels into their bodies, their bones, the screaming of the engines growing until the plane kicked upward, rotated and climbed steeply away from the runway.

"Noooooooo. . . ."

They were airborne.

14.

"I THINK we've leveled off," Pitch said. He had to yell to be heard over the engines, though they had cut back somewhat and were not quite as deafening. "Let's try to get more comfortable."

"This is not good," Hasty said. They wriggled and shoved until they were untangled and could at least sit upright. "Noise makes parrots smell more."

It was true. The parrots were at least as frightened as the boys, and the smell was becoming so thick they could have cut it.

"I'd give two weeks allowance for a flashlight." Pitch put his hands out and tried to feel where he was, and one of his fingers went into the bars of a toucan's cage. The bird rewarded him by pecking at his finger. "Ouch."

For a time the boys sat in miserable silence.

"Well," Hasty finally said, "are we having fun yet?"

"I'm sorry I got us into this," Pitch said. "It was stupid to get in the crate. You shouldn't have followed me."

"That's the story of my life." Hasty sighed, the sound lost in the noise of the engines. "Where do you think we're going?"

Pitch shook his head, forgetting that Hasty couldn't see him in the darkness. "I've been thinking about it and I don't think we'd be on a jet if we were going anywhere close. I think they only fly jets on long trips."

"Oh good."

"Oh good."

"What did you say?" Hasty asked.

"Nothing," Pitch answered.

"You copied me."

"I did not."

"Oh good."

"There, you did it again."

"I didn't either—it must be a parrot."

"Oh good."

"Oh good."

"Oh good."

When one of the birds started it seemed to open

up all the rest, and in moments the two boys couldn't get a word in sideways.

"Hello."

"Oh good."

"Hello."

"Hello."

Soon parrots were copying other parrots and at last Pitch could stand it no more.

"Shuttup," he yelled and of course that was the wrong thing to say. At least two birds and possibly three picked it up.

"Shuttup."

"Shuttup."

"Shuttup."

"WE'VE GOT TO MAKE A PLAN," Pitch yelled. "FOR WHEN THE PLANE LANDS."

"Oh good."

"Shuttup."

"WHAT HAVE YOU GOT IN MIND?" Hasty asked.

"Shuttup."

"Oh good."

The parrots rattled on while Pitch and Hasty thought. Hasty spoke first.

"We have to get out of this box," he yelled. "As soon after we land as possible."

Pitch nodded, again forgetting that Hasty couldn't see him. "It seems to be awfully strong." He poked the sides of the box. "He put it together with long screws. And the hatch where we got in locked tight when it closed."

"We could start yelling when we landed," Hasty said. "Just yell and yell. Maybe the parrots would even help us."

"I don't know. I don't think we should just yell. What if whoever is picking the crate up wherever we land is waiting right there? They could just take us away without any chance. I think we have to have more of a surprise."

"So you have a plan?"

"Sort of." Pitch leaned closer to Hasty to be heard over the sound of the engines and the screeching and yammering of the parrots. "After we land and when it looks right and everything is settled I think we should turn sideways in the crate and try to kick the side off and yell at the same time. I think if we hit it right we can break out. The main thing is to land running. If we're lucky at least one of us will get away. It all has to happen fast and be a surprise. That's our only hope."

"All right," Hasty yelled. "Just say when. . . ."

He was going to say more but the whine of the engines changed, decreased and became almost quiet.

"What's that?" Hasty said, fear in his voice. "What are they doing?"

The plane angled downward suddenly.

"I think they're beginning to descend to where they're going to land," Pitch said. "All right, get ready. Turn sideways."

They scootched around until they were sitting on the cages with their backs against one side of the crate and their feet against the other. The parrots went crazy, squawking and flapping in the cages.

The plane angled still more downward and there was an added clunking roar as the pilot lowered the landing gear.

"Get ready," Pitch said again, the noise rising around and inside the crate. "Get ready. . . ."

A mighty bounce hit the crate, followed by a smaller second bounce and a rumbling of the wheels on the runway as the plane touched down. The engines thundered once more and the plane slowed rapidly, throwing the boys to the front of the crate.

"We're taxiing," Pitch yelled.

The plane slowed still more, turned so sharply that the boys were pushed to the side, and the plane stopped.

Thumps.

More thumps.

The crate suddenly tipped, was lifted, then started to slide down at an angle. Another series of thumps.

"Now?" Hasty asked.

"No. Not yet. We have to get it just right. . . ."

The crate bounced, jerked sideways and rumbled up at an angle for a bit, then seemed to level off, trundling on something flat.

"Now?" Hasty asked again.

"Not yet. Hold it, hold it. . . ."

The crate hesitated for a moment, then tipped sharply downward and seemed to slide until it stopped with a bump.

They were sitting at a slight angle and there was a moment of stillness.

"Now!" Pitch yelled. "Now!"

And the boys yelled and kicked the side of the crate as hard as they could.

15.

"EEEAAAHHHH!"

Later Pitch thought about it and wished that he could have frozen the moment in time when they came out of the box. It was one of those things it would be better to remember when he was very old, sitting on a porch somewhere in a rocking chair. Yup, he would say to his grandchildren, and then there was the time we blew up the parrot crate. . . .

It was not what they did so much as where they did it. Pitch had thought to escape when the crate was in some storage room at the airport, the place where crates are usually picked up. Or perhaps on a loading dock outside the main terminal. When the crate stopped moving he thought they had arrived at the storage room or dock.

They were instead at the main baggage carousel in the baggage claim area in the lower level of the airport.

Surrounded by about two hundred and forty-seven people.

All of them waiting for their baggage.

One man, the smuggler who was waiting for the crate, tall with oily hair and wearing a smeared windbreaker jacket, actually had his hand out, touching the corner of the crate, ready to take it down and load it on a dolly he was holding, when the whole side of the crate exploded outward and two boys blew out screaming and yelling like madmen only to run over the unsuspecting crowd. What made it even worse was that most of the cages broke when they pressured the side out, and half the parrots and one very angry toucan also came barreling into the crowd.

Two people had to go to the hospital later for observation for shock. One of them passed out completely, face down on his garment bag. Two other people were bitten by the toucan. The first thing that hit most minds was that a bomb of some kind had gone off and almost all of them hit the floor instantly.

Pitch tripped over a businessman in a gray suit, came down in a forward somersault on top of a woman wearing a flowered dress, and flopped like a beached carp into a group of tourists from Maryland.

Hasty wasn't so lucky.

He had rolled to the right as he came out of the box. Somehow a parrot had glommed onto his hair and wouldn't let go. Hasty took a mighty leap off the edge of the carousel, screaming and trying to get the parrot out of his hair at the same time, and ran smack into the smuggler.

"What the . . . ?"

The smuggler went down but Hasty had too much forward movement to stop or even slow down. He bounced from side to side among several passengers who were in the process of dropping to the floor, tripped, and went head down into a waste container. Unfortunately the parrot went in first, and was plugged in the bottom by Hasty. The parrot went crazy trying to get out and Hasty had a bad three or four seconds.

"I felt like I was trying to kiss a grenade with feathers on it," he told Pitch later—much later—after the scratches had been healed.

There were three security police in the baggage area and they responded instantly.

Two of them grabbed Pitch, and one of them dragged Hasty out of the trash container. The loose parrots and the toucan found places to land and there was a moment of silence, everybody frozen in place, people lying on the floor, the boys being held by the airport security police. In the stillness the smuggler, realizing something was definitely wrong, started to run for the door.

"Stop him!" Pitch yelled. "He's a smuggler!"

"Hold it!" The security man who had helped Hasty pulled his revolver. "Right there. Everybody freeze until we figure it all out. . . ."

The smuggler stopped, raised his hands, and turned around.

The policeman looked at the two boys, the broken crate turning slowly around on the carousel, the parrots and toucans perched in the ceiling light fixtures, the smuggler standing with his hands in the air and two hundred and forty-seven people face down around the carousel.

"Start slow," he said to Pitch. "And tell me everything."

"Well, I was playing this pinball machine . . ."

"Where?"

"In Columbus."

"Columbus where?"

"Columbus, Ohio. I was playing this pinball machine in Columbus and a parrot said that something was wrong so we crawled through the ventilating system and found this crate, see, so . . ."

"Just a minute." Hasty stopped him and faced the

policeman. "Before he gets crazy—could you tell me where we are?"

"We're in the airport."

"No, I mean what town. You know. What city."

"Albuquerque."

"You mean New Mexico." Hasty said it as a statement, not a question, his face falling. "Albuquerque, New Mexico."

The policeman nodded.

"Is there any chance that we can be home by five-thirty?"

"You mean today? No chance."

Hasty sighed. "I am going to be grounded until I'm thirty-five years old. How am I going to tell my parents I'm in Albuquerque? I can't even spell it."

16.

PITCH AND Hasty were sitting on the library steps. Overhead the Saturday noon sun cooked down on them, made them lazy. They had been back a week and the scratches on Hasty's face had dried and were healing nicely. They had even washed most of the smell out of their hair.

"You know," Hasty said lazily. "I don't think we should do any more of these things."

"What things?" Pitch was almost not listening. He was looking across the street at something on the corner.

"These crazy things where we get into mysteries without really meaning to. There must be a million kids in the world who are just as happy without being like us. . . ."

"Oh, come on, it all turned out all right, didn't it?"

"Well . . ."

And it had. The smuggler in Albuquerque had cracked under questioning and the whole ring had been broken up and the smugglers arrested. It had been more extensive than Pitch and Hasty had realized. The ring covered seven states and two countries, and the police estimated that they smuggled nearly half a million dollars worth of rare birds a year—and all of it was brought down by Pitch and Hasty and their ride in the crate. Newspapers and television picked it up, calling the boys heroes.

Even the airlines got involved and gave them free rides back to Columbus the next morning, and a news magazine wanted to write their story.

"I guess it's all right," Hasty said. He leaned back in the sun, relaxed. "You're right. It did turn out okay, didn't it? I wonder what happened to the original parrot?"

"Hmmmm?" Pitch ignored him. He was openly staring across the street now, studying the hot dog cart on the corner.

"I said, I wonder what happened to the original parrot—the one that tipped us off in the first place? Hey, you aren't even listening to me." Hasty sat up. "What's the matter with you?"

"Nothing, really."

"Don't lie to me. I can tell when something is bugging you. What is it?"

"It's just that I've been watching that hot dog cart across the street and the guy is acting kind of weird."

"What do you mean?"

"Three people have come and bought hot dogs but he didn't take any money from them."

"So? Maybe he's just a generous hot dog seller. Maybe they're poor people and he's feeding them on his own. Maybe . . ."

"No. There's something funny going on. I can tell."

Hasty looked at him, looked across the street at the hot dog cart, then sighed. "I know what you're going to say next."

"What?"

"You're going to say that we ought to check it out."

"I mean you've got to admit it's pretty strange, him just giving away hot dogs. Maybe we ought to check it out."

Pitch stood up suddenly.

"What are you doing?" Hasty asked.

"It's about time for lunch. I feel like a hot dog." He started trotting down the steps. "You coming?"

Hasty watched him for a moment, then rose and followed.